# THE WOLF
# WHO CRIED BOY

For my good friends
Edward D. Higgins and Randall C. Harris

Copyright © 1989 by Jeffrey Dinardo. All rights reserved.
Published by Grosset & Dunlap, Inc., a member of
The Putnam Publishing Group, New York. Published
simultaneously in Canada. Printed in Singapore.
Library of Congress Catalog Card Number: 88-81174
ISBN 0-448-09314-6   A B C D E F G H I J

# THE WOLF
# WHO CRIED BOY

written and illustrated by Jeffrey Dinardo

PUBLISHERS   •   Grosset & Dunlap   •   NEW YORK

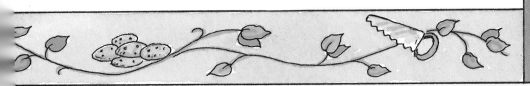

**O**nce upon a time there lived a young wolf who loved playing tricks.

One day the wolf was bored, so he took a stroll through the park.

From there he could see Mrs. Pig, Mr. Cat, and Mr. Turtle. They were all busy working in their shops.

"They are all so boring," said the wolf. "Let me play a trick on them."

Suddenly the wolf had an idea. He ran to the center of the park. He took a deep breath and yelled at the top of his lungs.

"Help!" he shouted. "There is a horrible little boy after me!"

Mrs. Pig dropped her pie.

Mr. Cat dropped his saw.

And Mr. Turtle almost
fell off his chair.

All three shopkeepers ran to the park. They found the wolf standing there.

"Where is that awful boy?" screamed Mrs. Pig.

"We'll save you from that beast!" yelled Mr. Cat.

"I'll call the police!" added Mr. Turtle.

The young wolf just laughed.
"I fooled you," he said. "There is no boy here.
I just played a trick on you!"

The shopkeepers were not amused.
"You should be ashamed!" said Mrs. Pig.
"You made me drop my saw!" said Mr. Cat.
"You are a naughty wolf!" added Mr. Turtle.

The shopkeepers angrily went back to their shops, leaving the wolf alone.

"That was so much fun," he thought. "Why don't I do it again!" So he ran to the pond.

The wolf took another deep breath and yelled as loud as he could.

"Help!" he screamed. "There is a horrible little boy after me!"

Mrs. Pig dropped
her tray of cookies.

Mr. Cat dropped his hammer.

And Mr. Turtle dropped
his favorite clock.

The three shopkeepers ran to the pond. There they found the wolf sitting on a rock, laughing.

"I fooled you all again!" he cried. "There is no boy here. It is just another joke!"

Mrs. Pig, Mr. Cat, and Mr. Turtle were angrier than before. They were also angry with themselves for being fooled twice.

"You are a scoundrel!" said Mrs. Pig.

"You should respect your elders!" said Mr. Cat.

"You are a naughty, naughty wolf!" added Mr. Turtle.

The three of them shook their heads as they returned to their shops.

"All this laughing has made me tired," said the
wolf, so he decided to take a nap. He lay down and
soon fell asleep.

Suddenly he heard a noise in the bushes and awoke.
"Who's there?" said the wolf.
But no one answered, so he closed his eyes again.

Then the wolf heard another noise. He sat up and said, "I am trying to sleep! Who is out there?"

Just then a head popped out of the bushes.
It had an ugly, scary smile on its face.

"I am a horrible little boy," said the creature,
"and I am after a nice juicy wolf!"

The wolf jumped up.

"Help!" he yelled. "There IS a horrible little boy
after me!"

But this time no one came.

"They don't believe you!" said the boy. "And now you are all mine!"

The wolf yelled again. He ran out of the park and did not stop running until he was all the way home.

Then the horrible little boy came out of the bushes ... and popped off his head. It was Mrs. Pig!

Out of the right arm came Mr. Cat. Out of the left arm came Mr. Turtle.

The three shopkeepers smiled at each other and went back to their shops.

Mrs. Pig finished baking her cookies.
Mr. Cat finished making his table.
Mr. Turtle repaired his favorite clock.
    And they were never bothered by that
young wolf again.